THIS WALKER BOOK BELONGS TO:

_____

_____

_____

_____

First published 1986 by Walker Books Ltd
87 Vauxhall Walk, London SE11 5HJ

This edition published 1998

Text © 1986 Allan Ahlberg
Illustrations © 1986 Colin McNaughton

This book has been typeset in New Baskerville Educational.

Printed in Hong Kong

British Library Cataloguing in Publication Data
A catalogue record for this book is
available from the British Library.

ISBN 0-7445-6127-2 (hb)
ISBN 0-7445-6075-6 (pb)

BEAR'S BIRTHDAY

Allan Ahlberg

Colin McNaughton

Bear's Birthday
Big Head
Open the Door

WALKER BOOKS
AND SUBSIDIARIES
LONDON • BOSTON • SYDNEY

Bear's
Birthday

a bear

a happy bear

a happy birthday bear

a happy birthday bear
and his friends

a party

a happy party

a happy noisy party

a sad noisy party

a sad noisy bear

a happy bear

tickle
tickle

a happy ending

Big
Head

big head little head

big ear little ear

big eye little eye

big nose little nose

big mouth   little mouth

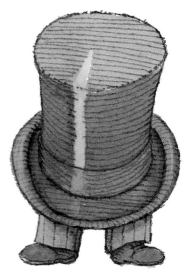

little hat   big hat

Open
the
Door

open the door

shut the door

open the window

shut the window

open the fridge

shut the fridge

open the box

shut the box

open the parcel

MORE WALKER PAPERBACKS
For You to Enjoy

Also by Allan Ahlberg and Colin McNaughton

RED NOSE READERS

Red Nose Readers are the easiest of easy readers – and the funniest!
Red for single words and phrases; yellow for simple sentences;
blue for memorable rhymes. How many have you got?

RED BOOKS

0-7445-1015-5	Bear's Birthday	£2.50
0-7445-1021-X	Big Bad Pig	£2.50
0-7445-1499-1	Fee Fi Fo Fum	£2.50
0-7445-1498-3	Happy Worm	£2.50
0-7445-1496-7	Help!	£2.50
0-7445-1497-5	Jumping	£2.50
0-7445-1014-7	Make a Face	£2.50
0-7445-1016-3	So Can I	£2.50

YELLOW BOOKS

0-7445-1700-1	Crash! Bang! Wallop!	£2.50
0-7445-1701-X	Me and My Friend	£2.50
0-7445-1020-1	Push the Dog	£2.50
0-7445-1019-8	Shirley's Shops	£2.50

BLUE BOOKS

0-7445-1703-6	Blow Me Down!	£2.50
0-7445-1702-8	Look Out for the Seals!	£2.50
0-7445-1018-X	One, Two, Flea!	£2.50
0-7445-1017-1	Tell Us A Story	£2.50

Walker Paperbacks are available from most booksellers, or by post from B.B.C.S., P.O. Box 941, Hull, North Humberside HU1 3YQ
24 hour telephone credit card line 01482 224626

To order, send: Title, author, ISBN number and price for each book ordered, your full name and address,
cheque or postal order payable to BBCS for the total amount and allow the following for postage and packing:
UK and BFPO: £1.00 for the first book, and 50p for each additional book to a maximum of £3.50.
Overseas and Eire: £2.00 for the first book, £1.00 for the second and 50p for each additional book.

Prices and availability are subject to change without notice.